William Edward Vasser

Flower Myths

And other Poems

William Edward Vasser

Flower Myths
And other Poems

ISBN/EAN: 9783337246556

Printed in Europe, USA, Canada, Australia, Japan

Cover: Foto ©Andreas Hilbeck / pixelio.de

More available books at **www.hansebooks.com**

FLOWER MYTHS

AND

Other Poems.

BY

WILLIAM EDWARD VASSER.

———

LOUISVILLE, KY.
PRINTED FOR THE AUTHOR BY JOHN P. MORTON AND COMPANY.
1884

TO THE MEMORY OF

MY DEAD FRIEND,

James Benagh Hobbs,

I INSCRIBE THIS LITTLE VOLUME—THIS "POOR FLOWER OF POESY."

"FOR SINCE IT PLEASED A VANISHED EYE,
I GO TO PLANT IT ON HIS TOMB ;
THAT IF IT CAN, IT THERE MAY BLOOM,
OR DYING, THERE AT LEAST MAY DIE."

CONTENTS.

FLOWER MYTHS.

I.

A country house embowered in stately trees,
With grassy lawn and flower embellished walks;
A rippling brook meandering through the grounds,
By rustic bridges spanned, and dashing o'er
Artistic piles of moss-incrusted rocks,
In picturesque cascades, whose cooling spray
Keeps fresh the lacy ferns through summer's heat :—
Imagine these, and you will have the scene
Of this, the masque, or sport, or what you will,
That makes the subject of our narrative.
The *dramatis personæ* are but few,
Embracing but one little family—
A widowed mother and four noble sons
And daughters twain, exquisite blossoms both.
Their father, years ago, had bravely drawn
His sword and marched forth at his country's call;
And while the laurels, well deserved for deeds
Of valor, clustered thick about his brows,

He fell in battle, and with dying breath
A message sent unto his loving wife,
A wish that she would not her days devote
To bootless sorrow, mourning o'er his fate,
Nor, clad in somber weeds, forever wear
A woeful aspect; but, resigned to fate,
Learn to subdue her grief, if that might be,
And feel or feign a cheerfulness, that she
Might make their children happy for his sake.
This admonition well had she observed.
All arts she used to hide the pangs of grief
That rent her heart, as tigers, in their lair,
Rend and devour their prey.   She gave her sons
Encouragement and help daily to store
Their minds with knowledge; taught them to perform
With willing hearts their labors; drew them on
To noble aims, and strove to shape their lives
In lofty molds.   She oft to them would say,
" The Surreys, Sidneys, Crichtons are not gone
From out the earth.   Though tourneys pass away,
And courtly *fêtes* no longer rule the hour,
'T was not the glamour of the lists and courts
That made the peerless knight, but 't was the MAN;
And manhood still as perfect may be made ;
And breasts as true as ever camis wore

May be concealed in homely, modern clothes,
And deeds as tender, brave, and knightly, now
May be performed, as ever graced the reign
Of spotless Arthur, or of Charlemagne."
Her daughters too, by nature well endowed,
Were trained in every fascinating grace
And indistinguishable art that makes
The charm of woman; taught to rule themselves
Firmly, and each unworthy passion tame,
And only freedom give to such desires,
Feelings, emotions, as may best become
The gentler sex. She taught them charity;
Not only that which gives but that which loves;
And all polite attainments that refine
And elevate and polish they possessed.
But not alone was self-improvement made
The children's aim, for they were also taught
The duty due to others, and with that
To keep, when fortune frowns, as when she smiles,
A cheerful mind. 'T was not enough, she said,
The stars should rise, but they should also shine
To beautify the night. No flower performs
Its functions fully by its growth alone,
But it must show bright colors and exhale
Its pleasing scents to add to earth's delight.

Thus ceaselessly did this sagacious dame,
This loving mother, strive by every wile,
By every innocent art to woman known,
To lure her children on those pleasant paths
That lead to virtue, wisdom, happiness;
And, both to entertain and to instruct,
She taught them plays and sports and merry masques.
And so it chanced that, on a summer day—
A lazy, drowsy day in summer, when
The agile squirrels ceased to clamber up
And down the trees, but hid them in the leaves,
And birds that sang so cheerily at dawn
Flew silently from shady bough to bough,
And all the family had gathered there
Upon the porch, where hung Madeira vines
Whose creamy, plume-like blossoms, lightly stirred
By gentle zephyrs, shed a rich perfume—
The mother's eyes o'erlooked the varied flowers
That filled the plots and fringed the gravel walks.
And these suggested to her mind a thought
She thus expressed: " To-morrow let us lunch
Beside the brook, beneath the Giant Beech;
And let us each impersonate some flower,
And tell in rhyme its origin, as learned
From history, tale, or famed Ovidian song.

What say you, children?"   With one voice they all
Declared the fancy excellent, and set
Their wits to wondering which of all the tales
Of human creatures turned to flowers they liked
The best; and soon each one had made a choice.
The eldest, Albert, chose the *Hyacinth.*
Matilda, just arrived at womanhood,
Preferred the *Rose,* because she loved it most,
And knew of it a quaint and charming tale.
The handsome Laurence, shapely, graceful, tall,
With Grecian face, and snowy skin, and eyes
Of darkest brown, and hair of kindred hue,
Would be *Narcissus,* famed for vanity;
But Arthur said that he would also be
Narcissus, though another sort of youth,
And quite a contrast to the self-loved boy.
Elizabeth, or Elsie, as they called
The youngest girl—a bright, vivacious maid—
Chose the gay *Sunflower,* much affected now
By fashion's throng, of whom but few can guess
Why Æsthetes make it their especial flower.
And little Walter, only twelve years old,
Youngest and best-beloved, quick, witty, gay,
Who, like a sunbeam, shone where'er he went,
And danced like Pau-Puk-Keewis every where,

Declared he knew no musty classic lore,
But said he'd make a story for himself
About the "*Johnny-Jump-Ups*"—so he called
The motley *Pansies*, droll as harlequins.
"And what will mother be?" asked one and all.
She faintly smiled, while in her breast a pain
Was gnawing, like the fox the Spartan hid,
And said that she would be the *Laurel*, first
Of all the flowers, and suiting best her age
Because of all the dignity it hath.
And so that drowsy day at once was filled
With sprightly talk and preparations brisk,
And charming labors, done with hearts as light
As those of harvesters who think upon
The feast and frolic of the Harvest-Home.

II.

Had Watteau's eyes beheld that rural scene
Of gayety—that bright, fantastic group,
Attired as flowers, there gathered by the brook,
Beneath the beech tree's verdant canopy,
Around a rustic board, with tempting meats
And fruits and cakes and ices well supplied,
It might have shone on fadeless canvas now.

And had Boccaccio heard the stories told
Of how they chanced to come into the world,
They might have been to far posterity
Sent down, preserved by his enchanted pen.
No art of mine can paint, in words, the scene:
Enough for me, in verse, to reproduce
The story, song and jest that sparkled there. . . .

The feast removed, the table decked with flowers,
And fragrant wines in moderation quaffed,
First, Albert, clad in Grecian garb, with wreath
Of artificial hyacinths bedecked,
(Their season long ere this had passed away),
And garlands hanging from his shoulders broad,
Stood forth, with iron quoits in hand, and told
In modern rhyme this ancient Grecian myth :

> The youth Hyacinthus, beloved by Apollo,
>   The quoits with that deity threw ;
> Apollo, with vigor surpassing a mortal's,
>   His discus discharged, and it flew
>   High into the clouds, where it blended
>   With them for awhile, then descended.
>
> The beautiful stripling, the quoit to recover,
>   To where it was falling then flew ;
> But, rebounding with force, in the forehead it struck him,
>   And the too daring mortal it slew ;

And soon to the earth he was sinking,
His life-blood the thirsty sod drinking.

Apollo, transported with grief, would have made him
    At once an Immortal above,
Had not the decrees of Olympus forbidden;
    And so, to betoken his love,
        He made of the blood of the fated
        This flower with its purple blooms freighted.

In letters invisible now to us mortals,
    He wrote on each petal "Alas!"——
"Alas!" for such beauty so destined to wither,
    And out of existence to pass;
        "Alas!" for the youth he would cherish,
        Yet doomed so untimely to perish.

When yearly fair Spring, whose light, snowy prætexta
    With hyacinth's purple is bound,
Is passing away, and the Sun-god of Summer
    Pours down his fierce rays on the ground,
        Killing all the fair flowers that are growing,
        Its sense then this fable is showing.

"Ah, ha! And so there is a meaning in it,"
The mother said; "The ancients often taught
Philosophy in fables such as this.
Matilda, you shall next be heard. How came
The roses in the world? Were they not made
In Nature's morning, by divine command?"
Matilda, decked and blushing like a rose,

From where she sat upon a rustic bench
Began to speak, low-voiced, with modest mein:

"How came the roses in the world?
    What caused them first to blow?
Were they not born in Nature's morn
    When flowers were made to grow?"

Tradition tells another tale:
    In Bethlehem afar,
In that blest land o'er which did stand
    The Magi's guiding star,

A maiden was accused of crime,
    Though guiltless she of blame,
And hers the doom, in youthful bloom,
    To die the death of shame,

They bound her to the dreadful stake
    And heaped the fagots high,
And lit the pile, with curses vile,   .
    And mocking sign and cry.

The maiden spoke no word to them,
    Nor strove to break the cord;
With lifted eyes and touching cries
    She called upon the Lord:

"O thou who hearest every prayer;
    On whom my hope is stayed;
To thee I bow,—have mercy now
    Upon a helpless maid!

" Oh, to these men a token give,
　　A token and a sign
That I have not, as thou dost wot,
　　Offended law of thine ! "

The prayer was heard, the fire was quenched,
　　And of each smoking brand
A branch was made, with flowers arrayed,
　　Unknown in any land.

The brands that had not taken fire
　　Were filled with roses white,
And those that caught were richly fraught
　　With roses ruby bright.

Aye, some did blush with crimson flush
　　For innocence reviled;
And some did blow, as white as snow,
　　For virtue undefiled !

" Where read you that, Matilda?" Albert asked.
And, smoothing down her leaves, the " Rose" replied:
" In Mandeville, the pioneer of prose
In England; whose rough strokes prepared the way
For smoother pens; who, frontier-tradesman-like,
Imported there a strangely-varied stock
Of facts and fancy—superstitious tales
And truthful observations from abroad.——
But where's Narcissus?   Let us hear from him."
That handsome youth, becomingly attired,

With ambling gait betook him to the brook   [limbs
That flowed hard by, and stretched his well-turned
Upon the grass, and, leaning o 'er the stream,
Surveyed his features in its limpid tide,
Then, lifting up his head, declaimed these lines:

Narcissus, the handsomest stripling in Greece,
   Impervious appeared to the arrows of love;
   Though thickly they flew, all unscathed did he move,
No amorous emotions disturbing his peace.

Sweet Echo pursued him through thicket and grove,
   Repeating his name in the tenderest tone,
   But, scorning her pleading, he left her alone,
To die in the forest, distracted with love.

To punish so heartless and ruthless a one,
   Stern Nemesis ordered, when next he should see
   Himself, of himself he enamored should be,
And die of his passion, as Echo had done.

So it happened one day, that, all hot from the chase,
   He came to a fountain and knelt by its brink,
   And, bending him over its waters to drink,
He saw there reflected his beautiful face.

His eyes were like stars, so the poets aver;
   As bright as the sun did his countenance glow;
   His cheeks were the blending of roses with snow;
His locks such as Bacchus' anointed with myrrh.

Enamored straightway, he was filled with unrest ;
  He courted his image, he called to it oft,
  And begged it, with utterance tender and soft,
To leave the cold fountain and dwell in his breast.

He smiled in its eyes, and its lips smiled again ;
  Allured by delusions enchanting as this
  He fondly endeavored the image to kiss,
But, touching the water, it vanished amain.

There long did he tarry, and often he sighed,
  Till, wasted and weary, at length he forsook
  The fair, cruel nymph that would stay in the brook,
And, stretching himself by its margin, he died.

From their home in the fountain the Naiads then came
  And bore him away to their grottoes below ;
  But there, on the spot where he perished, did grow
The saffron-hued flower that is called by his name.

" The more familiar legend that, 't is true,"
Said Arthur ; " but I 've read a prettier one,
A purer one, more delicate ; to which
Your coarser narrative compareth like
Some lurid bonfire blazing in the night
To that fair star which, trembling in the east,
Rosily glimmers in the dawning's flush.
But hear my version first and then decide."
And stepping lightly to the water's side,
Where grew a tuft of late Narcissus plants,

He sat beside them, toying with their blooms,
And told his story, speaking as to them:

> Why bend above the water's brim?
>   Why gaze intently in the stream?
> To mark the silver graylings swim,
>   Or note the giddy ripples gleam?
> Ah no; you gaze perforce to see
>   Reflected there your blooms of gold
> Obeying that divine decree
>   Made by the pitying gods of old.
>
> Narcissus roamed the Grecian fields,
>   His loved twin sister by his side;
> They plucked each flower the meadow yields,
>   Fair as themselves, and dewy-eyed.
> One scarce might tell the twain apart,
>   So like they were in form and face;
> Attired alike, alike in heart,
>   They rode together to the chase.
>
> But now, alas! the maid is dead,
>   And broken-hearted is the lad;
> The grasses grow above her head,
>   And he must evermore be sad:
> No more the hunt engages him;
>   The *fêtes* and games he now evades;
> He shuns the winecup's glowing brim,
>   Nor dances with the laughing maids.
>
> Hark! Echo calls: The hills in sport
>   Alone make answer to her call;
> In vain her tones his favor court,
>   Unheeded on his ear they fall;

The Naiad now, for her delight,
  Must seek a lover otherwhere,
He cares not if her breast be white,
  Nor dallies with her glossy hair.

He nurses by the water side
  A brother's love and deep despair,
And bends above the glassy tide
  To catch the image mirrored there;
(So like the object of his love!)
  Until he pined away and died
He came each day to bend above
  That lovely picture in the tide.

Their love and sympathy to show,
  The gods devised a graceful plan,
And caused beside the stream to grow
  A flower which seemed itself to scan:
And thus the pale Narcissi tell
  The tender thought, the passing grace
Of one who loved a sister well
  And in his image sought her face.

A controversy then among them rose
Concerning which account deserved the palm.
The ladies all, and little Walter, thought
The latter version prettier by far;
But Albert joined with Laurence and declared
It followed not the vein of classic myths.
The argument had likely waxed too warm,
Had not the mother with her usual tact

Invoked the *cloture* power, and called upon
" The mad Clytie " to render her account.
Elizabeth, so dark of hair and eyes,
Was gayly dressed in petticoat of brown,
With yellow overskirt, in petals cut,
And bodice brown, with collar sunflower-like,
While on her head, above her tresses bright,
A hat sat slanting to the setting sun,
Of sunflower shape, in brown and golden stuff.
She held in hand an imitation lyre ;
And Laurence deftly on his soft guitar
Struck up the chords her fingers seemed to wake,
While she, affecting much abandon, sang
To an old tune this ditty brief and wild :

How fair and grand the god Apollo !
  How sweet the music of his lyre !
The nymph Clytie his steps might follow
  From morn to night and never tire.

The nymph Clytie his steps did follow—
  Where'er they led she wildly went ;
She madly loved the great Apollo,
  To follow him she was content.

In vain the maids, protesting mildly,
  Bade her forsake the path he trod ;
She listened not, nor stayed, for wildly
  She did adore the beauteous god.

Though he, such lowly homage spurning,
    To notice her would never deign,
Yet back she never thought of turning,
    Nor cared for weariness nor pain.

But it was hard his course to follow,
    He was so swift of step, you see;
So, mad with love of great Apollo,
    At length she died—the poor Clytie!

He made her then, the good Apollo,
    A sunflower, that, with lifted eyes
And turning head, she still might follow
    His glorious journey through the skies.

"And so, because Apollo was the god
Of Art, and of the Muses president,
The Æsthetes wear the sunflower as a badge
Appropriate to Art's ardent followers;
And mad as Clytie some of them appear!"
The mother said; then Master Walter bade
Proceed to tell the story he had made.
That cunning lad, in comic masquerade,
A grotesque likeness to a pansy bore:
His slender form, in closely fitting suit
Of green, appeared much like a flower-stalk;
And on his head he wore a hood or cap
With flaps like pansy petals standing up
In front; above, one made of purple stuff

Beside another colored palest blue;
On either side the head were other flaps
Protruding; and, beneath his dimpled chin,
The points to which his yellow collar came
Made other petals; in this frame was set
His face, which wore the look of blank surprise
That pansies have.   With many gestures droll
And comic antics he declaimed his rhyme:

At the court of a king
'T was the commonest thing
  A motley fool to see;
And he quizzed every one
(For the king loved his fun)
  Except his Majestie.

And there always was seen
In a palace, I ween,
  A great magician too;
And he never did aught
But the things he thought
  The king would have him do.

And I never yet heard
Of a king so absurd
  As not to have a girl;
For it sorely would fret
Him an ally to get
  Without that " priceless pearl. "

So it chanced on a time
That a king in his prime
   Possessed these treasures three,
Viz., a jester, named John,
A magician, Luzon,
   And a daughter fair to see.

And this king he had planned
With his daughter's fair hand
   An ally strong to buy;
For he dreaded a war
Which he fancied he saw
   Within the future nigh.

To a neighboring king
He had mentioned the thing
   With all desired success,
But he did n't then know
Of a queer thing or so
   Which none, indeed, could guess.

It was nothing but this:
The precocious young miss,
   A passion strange possessed.
She had fallen in love,
By the powers above!
   With the jester, and not in jest.

And the jester returned
The passion that burned
   Within her bosom fair;
And they managed to meet
In a hidden retreat
   To do their courting there.

The magician one day
Heard the princess say
  "John, hide among the grass
To the right of the fir;
And you must n't dare stir,
  Though steps should near you pass.

"There I 'll come while they sup,
Saying 'Johnny, jump up,'
  By which you 'll know 't is me."
The magician then flew
To the king, who he knew
  In dudgeon high would be.

When the king was apprised,
The magician advised
  They should an example make
Of the jester so bold,
And a plan did unfold
  To make all jesters quake.

When the king had agreed,
They did quickly proceed,
  And severely the princess chid;
Then the court all stole out
In a circle about
  The spot where Jack was hid.

Then Luzon in his robes,
With his magical globes,
  And some concoction black
In a glittering cup,
Saying, "Johnny, jump up,"
  Approached the crouching Jack.

At the sound of the words,
Like a covey of birds,
　Uprose the motley wight;
Then the king shook his fist,
And the courtiers all hissed
　And mocked his wretched plight,

Crying, "Johnny, jump up!
For his Highness doth sup!"
　And then they jeered and laughed.
And the dreadful Luzon
Straight emptied upon
　His head the magic draught,

And he dwindled away
To the size of a fay
　And changed into a flower,
Agape, and with eyes
Enlarged by surprise,
　Appearing to this hour;

And his asses' ears blue*
Into petals then grew
　That framed his face within;
And his collar of buff
Made him petals enough
　To hang beneath his chin.

And wherever he grew
All the jesters well knew
　'T was not the safest thing
So absurd e'er to prove
As to venture to love
　The daughter of a king!

---

* The caps of court jesters of old were adorned with asses' ears.

Much merriment did Master Walt. provoke,
And diverse comments on his rhyme were made.
Some thought it libel on the pansies, thus
To give them such an origin absurd;
And some declared they did n't look at all
Grotesque to them, the ladies waxing wroth.
One quoted Poe, who calls them " Puritan ;"
Another, Shakespeare's often quoted line,   [said
" There 's pansies—that 's for thoughts;" and so they
Their very name was from the French for " thought."
But Walter bravely battled for his own
Conception of the pansy's origin
With many a witty argument, and vowed
The tale was quite as true as all the rest.
At last, all, wearying of the hopeless task
Of winning over that perverse young mind,
Desired to hear the mother tell in verse
The Laurel's origin. She was attired
In glossy satin gown of darkest green,
With laurel leaves becomingly adorned;
A laurel wreath encircling her fair brow.
In faltering voice she sang the laurel's praise,
And told its tale in alternating strains:

The Laurel tree, the Laurel tree !
It lifts its boughs in majesty.
Oh how the bosom proudly heaves
Of him who wears its glossy leaves !
Of all the earthly trees that grow
No other one is worshiped so.

Apollo was wounded, ah yes, to his sorrow,
  By Cupid, designing his power so to prove,
Who chose for the purpose a gold-headed arrow
  Which, piercing the bosom, transports it with love.

Before the laurel tree was made,
The Grecian boy who best displayed
His swiftness, strength, or gift of speech,
Was proud to wear the crown of beech ;
But when the laurel sprang to life
Its leaves alone inspired the strife. .

Fair Daphne forthwith was beloved by Apollo ;
  But Cupid, in mischief, an arrow of lead
Let fly at her bosom ; from which it did follow
  That, hating her lover, before him she fled.

The warrior draws his shining blade
And braves the deadly cannonade,
And proudly treads the bloody field,
Resolved to die, but never yield,
Nor place his weapon in its sheath
Until he wins the laurel wreath.

The swiftly pursuing Apollo alarmed her ;
  But, hearing and heeding her desperate prayer,
The gods to a Laurel that instant transformed her,
  Her body to wood and to foliage her hair.

The bard, the rosy draught of health,
The joys and luxuries of wealth,
Resigns without a moan or sigh,
Content obscure to live and die,
If Fame upon his coffin weaves
Her fadeless wreath of laurel leaves.
Apollo, the Laurel in rapture embracing
  (A wreath of its leaves ever after he wore),
Decreed that, the brows of the worthiest gracing,
  An emblem of fame it should be evermore.

How swift the hours roll by when nimble wits
Tug at their wheels, and oil them with the flow
Of sparkling fancies and enchanting tales!
These rhymes and songs and pleasing fantasies,
And much beside that I have left untold,
So charmed that merry company that, ere
They thought the afternoon half passed away,
'T was time for all to hie them to the house.
For now the evening clouds were streaked with red;
And, shooting forth his most resplendent rays,
The glorious sun rode down the western sky,
A warrior, slow retiring from the field
His arms have won, all stained with crimson gore,
While round him flash a thousand golden spears!

OTHER POEMS.

OTHER POEMS.

THE LION, DEMOCRACY.

The myrmidons of ruthless tyranny
  Who seek this lordly lion's limbs to bind,
  The slaves of gold who wish him well confined
That they may work their will at liberty,
Should dread his wrath, and shun him fearfully;
  But they whose bosoms never have designed
  To do him wrong will ever find him kind
As Una's tawny friend; though, verily,
When rash and ravenous enemies have planned
  His capture, while asleep he seemed to be,
Palm-shaded and by Freedom's breezes fanned,
  His teeth have gleamed, and lightnings lit his eye,
And, tempest-mouthed, with roars he shook the land,
  As up he leaped—the fierce Democracy!

(33)

O'DONNELL.

The red hand of murder I take not in mine,
　And treacherous plotting, I never can praise it;
But truth I will honor where'er it may shine,
　And courage delights me, whoever displays it!
As black as a demon's unfrequented haunt
　That breast which beholds, without pity or sighing,
A hero whose land is oppressed and in want,
　For love of his people and liberty, dying.

The nations of Europe rejoice in their strength,
　And nothing they reck if the weaker ones perish;
To spread their dominion they pause at no length,
　And little of justice or mercy they cherish.
Poor Turkey to Russia must truckle and bow;
　The hist'ry of Poland 's the saddest e'er written;
And Ireland's emerald bosom is now
　All torn by the lashes of merciless Britain.

Ah, Erin! thy country was fertile of old—
　But none of its harvests are given the toiler;
The yield that is gathered in bread or in gold
　But battens and strengthens thy despotic spoiler.

Like storm-driven birds, from the land of their birth
    Thy children are borne by oppression and danger,
Their genius, their valor, their wit and their worth
    To lay at the feet of a foe or a stranger.

But sad as the wreck of a people may be,
    Downtrod in the march of another to glory,
Far sadder and bitterer still 't is to see
    The neck of one man 'neath a nation's foot, gory.
A court is a temple, an ægis, the law,
    But not for an Irishman ægis or temple,
If England should choose, in her tyrannous war,
    On justice and statutes to ruthlessly trample.

O'Donnell, the martyr, his sentence received,   [him,
    And bore him in death as tho' nothing had pained
For the arms of invisible angels that grieved,   [him.
    And the love of his people upbore and sustained
But England shall learn that the death of a man
    Illegally taken, in fear or vainglory,
But sets on her scepter a curse and a ban,
    And blots with a murder this page of her story !

She boasts that the sun never sets on her lands—
    Its circling can bring to her empire no morrow ;

But reeking with innocent blood are her hands,
   And tears wash her feet with an ocean of sorrow.
Her kingdom must crumble to ashes some day,
   Her realm be divided, her scepter be broken,
For vengeance is God's, and He 'll surely repay—
   The wicked must perish, for so He hath spoken.

COMPARISONS.

Is it best to be one of a garden of flowers
  That blossom in freedom from cover and wall,
Where butterflies flit in the sunniest hours
  And lightly pay court to the charms of them all,

Or best to be only a separate flower
  That gladdens a house where it blossoms alone,
Yet blossoms not only in sunniest hour,
  But cheers and is cherished when summer has flown?

Is it best to be one of a concert of songs
  Whose varying melodies ravish the ear,
And puzzle the listeners who gather in throngs
  To tell which is sweetest of all that they hear,

Or best to be only a separate song
  Whose resonant harmonies lighten and swell
The heart of a toiler and render him strong
  To shoulder his burden and carry it well?

Is it best to be one of a bevy of maids,
  Light-hearted and joyous in youth's sunny days,

Admired ere the bloom of their loveliness fades
   By gallants who court them with meaningless praise,

Or best to be only a dutiful wife,
   With cares which the bosoms of wives ever hold,
But loving and loved through the years of her life
   With love that is boundless and never grows cold?

TO ADELAIDE,

WITH FLOWERS, ON HER RETURN AFTER A SUMMER'S ABSENCE.

Adelaide, I have culled for your pleasure these flowers,
Whose beauty has lingered through all the dull hours
Of all the long summer, to keep in my mind
Your flower-like beauty and graces refined
As subtlest aroma of jasmine or rose,
Or whatever blossom 's the sweetest that blows.
As lovely reminders of loveliness lost
They stood in my garden, like sentries on post,
Through all your long absence, and whispered, in
So soft and so tender that I, and the birds   [words
That nestled among them, alone could make out
Their meaning, and all they were talking about,
As, weeping at morning, they grieved for a face
No more to be seen in its usual place,
And, drooping at evening, they sadly would say
"The Queen of all blossoms continues away!"
Geraniums, as bright as the blush on your cheek
When vainly I struggle your praises to speak;
The bells of the fuchsia that gracefully nod,
Elastic and light as your step on the sod;

And roses—some white as your brow (brighter far
Than the brow of an Houri illumed with its star),
And some of them red as the hue of your lips,
That are red as the juice of the grape as it drips
From presses in Provence; all these, yea, and more,
Have wept and have drooped, and have mourned o'er
      and o'er
Your absence to me, when I sought them to trace
A sign of thy spirit, a hint of thy face
In petal and tendril of blossom and vine,
Whose beauties suggested the charms that are thine.
And now, in reward for this service well done,
I lovingly, tenderly, gather each one,
And send them to bloom in your presence divine—
To bourgeon and blow in a sweeter sunshine
Than any that ever has gladdened our town
Since *their* sun and *mine* on my garden went down.

A FALLEN IDOL.

High-niched within the temple of my heart
    An idol stood, all faultless in my sight:
The rosy tint it wore in love's warm light,
    Its pose, *finesse de grain*, and every part
Proportioned fitly by the sculptor's art,
    Combined, it seemed, as seen from its great height,
To make a form divine; and day and night
    My soul to it did adoration pay;
Till lo! in time, it fell upon the ground,
    And right before my feet it broken lay,
When, scanning it amazedly, I found
    'T was but a coarse and faulty piece of clay!
My partial sight alone had made it seem
    A work full meet to fill a master's dream.

4

SERENADE.

The musk-rose, love, is sweetest now,
  The evening star hath risen;
The closing flower a tardy bee
  Hath caught and shut in prison.
And now the moon, on silvery shoon,
  Ascends the slopes of blue,
And sheds her light, dear maid, this night
  To brighten paths for you!

Oh, love, there's music on the breeze!—
  To soothe his mate to slumber
The feathered minstrel fills her bower
  With many a tuneful number!
And hark, afar, a soft guitar
  And voices sweet and clear!
Your breast, I know, will softer grow
  When strains like these you hear!

Oh, come, fair girl, and walk with me
  These paths like silver glowing,
And fill with music's honied draught
  Thy soul to overflowing;

And lend thine ear again to hear
  The tale I would repeat,
Of how my soul were freed from dole
  If thou wert mine, oh sweet!

AT MY BROTHER'S GRAVE IN WINTER.

The air is chill; the frost's white hand
    Has silvered o'er each prostrate blade.
Of russet grass; the cedars stand
    In dark habiliments arrayed,
Like stricken mourners, round the bed
Where lies in everlasting sleep my unforgotten dead.

The maple lifts its branches bare
    Against the chilly, winter sky;
And snow-birds perch upon them there,
    Too cheerless or too cold to fly;
And, near a clump of blackened briars,
A rabbit seeketh stealthily the food that it desires.

I like the stillness of the time;
    I like the frosty air that stings
My tingling cheeks; for well the prime
    Of winter and the blight it brings
Accord with this unceasing pain
That, worse than winter, chills my heart and dully
        throbbing brain.

When leaves were on that maple tree,
   And mocking-birds, through summer days,
In strains of varied minstrelsy,
   Poured out their tuneful roundelays,
And grasses flourished, thick and green,
And flowers of all enchanting hues on every hand
     were seen,

'T was then his life, whose hand had clasped
   My own so oft, was snatched away,
Before my startled lips had gasped
   " Brother, farewell ! " or I could pray
Forgiveness from that tender heart
Which I, in boyish petulance, had often made to
     smart.

Oh, how I hated then the blush
   Of roses gladdening other eyes,
And all the splendors of the flush
   That lit the summer sunset skies,
Because his beauty-loving mind,
Enveloped in eternal night, to all their glow was
     blind.

And how I hated every song,
   When birds, from out their joyous throats,

In fitful strains, now soft, now strong,
   Poured forth around their varied notes,
Because his music-loving ear
Was deaf to all their melody, nor any strain could
     hear.

But in this season, meet for grief,
   Of desolation and decay,
My troubled spirit seeks relief,
   And sadly to myself I say,
" 'T is well that he is lying low,
   Where he can neither feel its breath, nor hear the
     tempest blow."

But surely I his traits forget;
   Such words are, like my sorrow, vain;
His spirit hardships did not fret;
   He took but little heed of pain;
For he adorned our manly race,
Who hold it brave to scorn distress—to shrink
     from it, disgrace.

'T was *I* who feared the wintry storm;
   'T was I who sighed for orange trees
And tropic arbors, where, in warm
   And spicy airs, I might at ease

Recline on beds of lilies white
And conjure up poetic dreams—a pampered sybarite.

But he rejoiced in hardy sports,
   The fiery steed, the wildest game,
The mimic fight in fields and forts,
   That filled the village with his fame;
And he revered, as priests their creeds,
Our soldier-brothers' memories—the blazon of their
     deeds.

And I remember perfectly,
   When we were both cadets at school,
How drear the barracks seemed to me,
   How harsh I thought the martial rule;
While he enjoyed the soldier life,
And ever smiled exultantly to hear the drum and
     fife;

And when the wintry night winds roared
   He often walked my post for me;—
When up the steps, with clanking sword,
   The sergeant came, and hurriedly
Pronounced my name, *he* caught the word,
And quickly rose to take my place, ere I the sum-
     mons heard.

How vain, how vain! to seek relief
   Of any season's bloom or blight
For aching hearts and poignant grief
   That neither change for gloom or light,
Nor lull for summer's balmy breeze,
Nor deaden for the frigid blasts that sway the
      naked trees!

I know, when yonder maple glows
   In gaudy suit of crimson flowers,
And, shaken by each breeze that blows,
   Upon his grave its petals showers,
When every tuft of withered grass
Erects again its tender blades to muffle steps
      that pass,

And when the flowers he loved the best
   Shall deck again his resting place,
And birds, returned from southern nest,
   Shall miss from earth his kindly face,
And, lighting by this grave of his,
For all the love he bore them, sing their sweetest
      threnodies;

I know my heart will still it sighs
   (Vain hope!) to hear his silvery voice,

To see again his soft brown eyes,
  And feel I never can rejoice,
  As once I could at any thing
Unless some power his vanished form again to life
    could bring!

THE JACQUEMINOT ROSE.

Full many a bloom our rosary contains,
   And varied colors do its blossoms show ;
But all are pale and dull and quite eclipsed
   Beside the full and flaming Jacqueminot.
As country lassie unto courtly dame,
As friendship's ray to passion's fervid flame,
     So other blossoms show
     Beside this rose's glow.

A ruby bright of wondrous hue and size
   It looks, when o'er it golden sunshine streams ;
The tinted Tea or pale Lemarque beside
   As pallid pearl or changing opal seems ;
Above their blooms it hangs upon its stem,
Each petal glowing like a brilliant gem,
     Like ruby necklace pressed
     Upon a snowy breast.

The butterflies about the Jacqueminot
   In rainbow circles flit or poise or light ;
Though other flowers as sweet of scent may be
   No other one can boast a hue so bright,

And only by a lustrous, dazzling sheen
Are color-loving insects drawn, I ween ;
    The flower of all most bright
    Doth give them most delight.

The Jacqueminot is like my Queen of Hearts,
    My crownèd Queen of many loving breasts ;
So bright she seems, so fair her queenly face,
    My charmèd spirit in her presence rests.
As moths desire the brightest star by night,
And butterflies by day the flower most bright,
    So does my soul desire
    My Queen, whom all admire.

BEN.

A tender heart, a kindly hand,
  A gentle, unassuming air,
  Are more desired, I think, and rare
Than brilliant parts and fortunes grand.

At least I know there is not found
  Among the gifted sons of men
  Who triumph with the sword and pen,
And with the laurel leaves are crowned,

The strong, mesmeric tie that binds
  My soul to one who may not claim
  The prestige due to place and fame
And mastery of giant minds.

The spell he weaves about our hearts
  Alone is found, and has its birth
  In admiration of his worth
And in the faith that worth imparts.

His will subdues me, and I move
  Obedient to his kind command;

And when I err, his steady hand
Restores me to the wonted groove.

When gay companions bid me go
   Where Pleasure waits the Hours to crown
   With garlands bright, and reason drown
In wit and wine and music's flow,

His voice restrains me, and in haste
   He brings a cup of purer joys
   Whose draught delights but never cloys,
And leaves behind no bitter taste.

No ghost of care that haunts the mind,
   No lure of dark temptation born,
   But he can laugh its spell to scorn
And whistle it adown the wind.

Though fade it must, and wilted fall,
   I place this garland on his brow;
   And, musing on his nature, vow
That fame is naught, that worth is all;

And say, though flattery's lips should form
   For me her most seductive phrase,
   It still shall be my highest praise
That I have won his friendship warm.

BALLADS.

The miner digs the hidden gold
　From out the earth with pick and spade,
And when 't is shaped in proper mold,
　With proper stamp upon it laid,
　What once was hidden now is made
　The useful currency of trade.

The lapidary bathes a stone,
　And cuts it smooth and sets it fair
To deck some queen upon her throne,
　Or sparkle in some beauty's hair,
　And all the world that sees it there
　Is dazzled by its luster rare.

And so the ballads turn the gold
　Of old Romance to currency,
And set the gems of history old
　Where all their beauty can descry ;
　And every where, like coins, they fly,
　And charm, like jewels, every eye.

THE POET'S HONEYMOON.

OCTOBER.

" I know what your poem will be," she said,
  And laughed in his face as she reached her arms
  Up over his shoulders, and joined her palms,
And plaited her fingers behind his head.
  " 'T will be about roses all faded and fallen,
'T will be about grasses all yellow and dead,
  'T will be about heather in clusters of purple,
'T will be about leaves that are golden and red.
Say, truthfully, won't it ? Just answer me now !"
  And merrily twinkled her mischievous eyes,
While warm was the touch of her lips on his brow.

"A wonderful prophetess you, no doubt,"
  He answered her, laughing. " But you 'll agree
  A poem without them, this month, would be
Like Hamlet with Hamlet himself left out.
  Whoever would herald October's returning,
Her livery must wear and her colors hang out ;
  Tho' threadbare the trappings and ancient the colors,
'T is cruel the wearer and bearer to flout.
Now is n't it truly ? Just answer me this,"

He asked her, with passionate, loving embrace,
And sealed her red lips for a time with a kiss.

"Ah, well! but you'll sigh for the summer past,
   For butterflies gaudy and songs of birds,
   And mention in sorrowful, tender words
The blossom that lingers alone, the last;
   And plaintively murmur in pitiful verses
About the approach of the merciless blast,
   The snows and the blight and the wild desolation
That come with the winter that's coming so fast.
Say, honestly, won't you?   Now tell me the truth,"
   She asked him, and pouted, as though she believed
That poets were gloomy repiners, forsooth!

" No, never—I swear it!" he then replied.
   " Repine I will never, nor care a fig
   For vanishing blossom and leafless twig,
As long as my darling is at my side.
   The winter may bluster—I dread not his fury,
While, blest with affection, with you I abide,
   In summer or winter an Eden I find it—
An Eden where you like a seraph preside."
No poem was written—he lingered all day
   To feast on her charms, and the poem forgot—
And many a poem's forgotten that way.

TO AN ABSENT LADY.

The stars of night are bright, I own,
  But I care not if they go,
For at morn I see the eastern sky
  With roseate light aglow.

The summer flowers are fair indeed,
  All white and pink and blue ;
But autumn's leaves are brighter still
  With gold and crimson hue.

The birds of spring that blithely sing
  Make beautiful notes, I know,
But there's a grander melody
  When winter's trumpets blow.

O star that gave my only light !
  O blossom that cheered my path !
O bird that sang in a sweeter tone
  Than other music hath !——

For me a dark and dreary void
  Is left, now thou art gone ;
Of all earth's bright and lovely things
  I sigh for thee alone.

TO ADELAIDE,

WITH A NOSEGAY OF VIOLETS.

Of all the flowers that bloomed ere while
  But one is lingering yet;
It is my favorite of them all,
  The dainty violet.

I love it for its timid look,
  And for its azure hue;
It minds me of your modest air
  And of your eyes of blue.

It brings to mind your gentle self,
  So delicate and pure,
With head bowed down so gracefully—
  The violet demure.

TO ADELAIDE,

ON BEING REPROACHED BY HER FOR NOT SAYING MY PRAYERS.

". . . Nymph, in thy orisons
Be all my sins remembered."

The mildest of zephyrs that wake in the spring,
The softest of down on the cygnet's white wing,
The sweetest of odors the summer distills,
The purest of waters from crystalline rills,—
Whatever is chosen on earth or in air
Is reckon'd too base for a symbol of prayer.

A something so gentle that, wafted on high,
'T would match with the infinite peace of the sky;
A something so free from all blemish and stain
That Eden to welcome its presence were fain;
A something so sweet and immaculate, where
Shall we find, for a type and a symbol of prayer?

Then how shall a bosom that's hardened by wrong,
That's governed by passions ignoble and strong,
That's blackened by sin and embittered by strife
And stained with the dust of the battle of life,

Oh, how shall a bosom like mine ever dare
To offer to Heaven its impious prayer!

Do zephyrs awake in the land of the snow?
Shall holy desires in my cold bosom glow?
Do odors of roses in deserts abound?
Shall sanctified thoughts in my bosom be found?
Oh, how shall a heart that's of piety bare
Be filled with the voice or the spirit of prayer!

But *thine* is a conscience as clear as the day;
Thy yearnings are mild as the zephyrs of May;
Thy thoughts are as sweet as the breath of the flowers,
That cluster in Eden's bright, amaranth bowers;
Thy spirit's as pure as thy visage is fair,
And Heaven would smile as it answered *thy* prayer.

Oh, nymph! in thy orisons think of my name,
And pray that it never be sullied with shame!
That, knightly in honor, and saintly in trust,
It shine like a buckler untarnished with rust!
Unworthy I am thy devotions to share,
But, prithee, remember my name in thy prayer!

ALABAMA BEREFT.

SUGGESTED BY THE DEATH OF SENATOR GEORGE S. HOUSTON.

Well may'st thou weep, Cornelia of the South!
    For thou, indeed, hast lost a jewel son.
The Roman Gracchi were not so beloved,
    Nor with more worthy deeds their honors won.
Thy stalwart son deserves a Roman's fame,
    For Cato was not more supremely just,
Augustus was not wiser in the state,
    Nor Brutus truer to the people's trust.

The suave address, the smooth and oily tongue,
    His manly nature aye disdained to own;
His manner was as open as the day,
    And bold sincerity rang in his tone;
He never sought by crafty wiles to be
    The cynosure of admiration's gaze,
But with calm mein and blameless life he wore
    The people's gift—the crown of civic bays.

Well may his days seem all too few to thee—
    And yet he gave to time a perfect fame;

For, though death wrote the *finis* to his deeds
   While yet he strove to build a greater name,
Still, in the compass of his years, he had
   Achieved for thee, his loved and cherished State,
A full redemption; and from all thy woes
   A happy issue and a glorious fate.

All praise, all honor, to thy noble son!
   Who was the staff on which you sorely leant
When debt oppressed, and 'neath an alien yoke
   Thy queenly head in bondage vile was bent.
He was thy guide, and at his magic touch
   Thy debt was lifted and thy foes dispersed;
At his behest the clouds went rolling back
   And Freedom's sunshine on thy pathway burst!

Let others boast the softer arts to show;
   Let other gems the brighter polish claim;
But he was peerless for intrinsic worth,
   And his career was purest from all blame.
His only aim was still the people's good;
   He labored ever with a tireless arm
To save the fruits of industry and toil
   And shield the citizen from every harm.

Enduring honor to thy noble son !
Let memory keep his deeds from growing dim !
Let history shrine his virtues in her page !
Let all thy younger statesmen copy him !
Thou shalt not bear a greater one than he :
His massive mind and his herculean will
Shall stand as prodigies amid the years,
And to thy latest day be honored still.

LINES WRITTEN ON A FLY-LEAF OF TENNY-SON'S DRAMA, QUEEN MARY.

O Tennyson! thy genius hitherto
Hath seemed to burn with luster nebulous;
But now, methinks, it hath burst forth to shine
With full orbed splendor, and an astral light.
In fancy oft I 've seen your mystic muse
Shrouded in mists that rise in silvery clouds,
With eyes upturned in sweet and blissful thoughts,
Like one of Raphael's angels, rapt and pure!
But as the shadows of senescent night
Fall back before the morning's opal glow,
Or as the morn, veiling her roseate breast,
Flieth abashed before the face of day,
So shall those adumbrations of thy verse
Which thy fine fancy had so fairly wrought
(And yet so faintly that we scarcely knew
If it were more from weakness or design),
Pale into naught—eclipsed by the excess
Of splendor in this greater work of thine.
Thy drama stands, like a Corinthian shaft,
Strong and compact, yet polished and ornate,
Combining all most admirably well;
And thou hast wreathed it with thy fancy flowers
As chastely bright as Eden's asphodel.

THE POET'S FAME.

" I will sing no more to the heedless world,"
    The fameless poet said,
And into the waves his harp he hurled;
    And he clasped his hands
    By the white sea sands,
And he bowed his weary head.

He had touched all chords, he tried all strains,
    To wake the voice of praise;
And now in despair his soul complains
    That he has no art
    To enchant the heart,
And for him there grow no bays.

But lo! there comes to his side a maid,
    (The poet's love is she),
And upon his brow her hand is laid,
    And her soft eyes glow,
    As in accents low
She murmurs, "Sing to *me*."

Then the bard uprose with a burning brain
    And a flushed and shining face,

And he caught his harp from the ebbing main,
  And he sang a song
  Of his passion strong,
With a rich and golden grace.

He had ceased to dream of the laurel bough ;
  Of *her* alone he thought ;
And a sacred light suffused his brow
  While he sang of love,
  As though from above.
He an angel's voice had caught.

And his sweet love song thro' the wide earth spread
  Till all men knew it well ;
And it lived in their hearts when the bard was dead,
  For, where'er they strove
  To interpret love,
There its magic numbers fell.

O poet ! sing to the human heart,
  Nor seek to win a name.
'T is the crowning grace of the singer's art,
  That the closer he rests
  To human breasts,
The grander is his fame.

DANTE AT RAVENNA.

Look, where he comes! the black-browed Florentine!
  His step is slow—his eyes are on the ground,
But piercing through to regions subterrene!
  Just then he saw (that moment when he frowned)
Francesca and her lover, ruthless whirled
By sulphurous cyclones through the under world.

His path pursuing with a measured stride,
  Anon his lips, curled with a bitter sneer,
The torments of some helpless Guelph deride,
  For shrieks and groans are music to his ear:
And he delights to have each hated foe
Writhe in extremes of heat and cold below.

Poor exiled Dante! Oh, if hope's decay
  And luckless love and banishment from friends
Can e'er excuse the passions' lawless sway,
  Such dire mischance extenuation lends
To thy embittered speech and cynic sneer,
Which prince and prelate contemplate with fear.

But see his upward glance!—just where a beam
  Of sunshine through an open archway falls

Upon his path !   A thousand splendors gleam
   In his deep eyes, as though they were the halls
Where light and love and joy were wont to sport,
And rose-crowned ecstasy held endless court !

Those eyes a supernatural vision own,
   And to their gaze is peopled all the sky;
Heroes and saints upon the breeze are blown :
   And they behold, up in the zenith high,
His Beatrice o'er the throng preside,—
His early love, his spirit's only bride.

Oh, wondrous mixture of the stern and mild !
   Most fervid nature that the world e'er saw !
Oppression fills him with resentment wild !
   His love is constant as the reign of law :
And his bold fancy paints in vivid hues
The forms he loves to honor or abuse.

One day in Florence, many years ago,
   When he, a gay and brave Italian youth,
A guest was at a banquet of Folco,
   A maid he met, whose beauty was, in truth,
Surpassing—then were kindled in his breast
Fires that will burn forever without rest.

Long since the maiden passed to realms above,
   And soon he took a thrifty dame to wife;
But only Folco's daughter could he love,
   And she is still the guardian of his life:
His heart for her as ceaselessly will yearn
As doth the needle to the north-star turn.

And next to her he loves his mother land;
   He longs for peace among the jarring states;
And his true heart with joy would burst to stand
   Once more within his native city's gates.
But he is doomed to dwell in darkness here,
With naught but his great dreams his life to cheer.

Soon will he join his idol in the sky,
   Where he will find a sweet, abiding home;
And his shall be a fame that can not die,
   Though he be not with laurels crowned at Rome.
And thou Ravenna, boast this four-fold trust—
His cares, his dreams, his labors, and his dust!

"COME, SING ME A SONG."*

TO LUCIUS.

Come, sing me a song ere thy going,
  My Lucius, with eloquent eyes!
Come, sing to a heart overflowing
  With tenderness born of the skies.
The moonlight, descending so softly
  And bathing the world in its glow,
Of peace from above is a token
  To my weary spirit below.

My Lucius, thou light-hearted stripling!
  I see thou art eager to go
Where the laughter of maidens is rippling
  And the gay dancers flit to and fro.
But surely thou 'lt linger a moment
  And sing me the song I love best;
'T will blend with the charm of the moonlight,
  And lift every cloud from my breast.

---

* Those who do not remember the popular song entitled "How the
Gates Came Ajar," will not understand these verses; but the author
chooses to publish them for personal reasons.

Yes, sing of the bright, shining city,
  And "the little, white angel, May,"
Whose soul was possessed of such pity
  For some coarser creature of clay,
That with the old warden she pleaded
  Who guards that great doorway afar
(With hope that her loved one might enter)
  To leave the bright portal ajar.

My Lucius, 't is strange that a creature
  So hardened and sinful as I
Should love, like a saint or a preacher,
  To hear of that house in the sky;
But the spell of your music subdues me
  To moods that are pure as the snow,
And your sweet, tender melodies move me
  Till the soft tears, in spite of me, flow.

At times, as I travel this dreary
  And wearisome journey of life,
Of its infinite pain I am weary,
  And I long for an end to its strife:
But then when you come with your music
  And roll the dark shadows away
I fancy those heavenly portals
  May open for me at some day.

But Lucius, my boy, I detain you ;
   Go, dance with the fair ones who wait,
And say to them, should they constrain you
   To tell them what made you so late,
That you paused, like an angel of mercy,
   As you flew to their circle of light, ·
To give a sweet moment of pleasure
   To one who stood out in the night.

THE USE OF THE USELESS.

Nay, poet, shrink not so abashed
   Before the ruder workman's scorn;
The higher use, the greater good,
   Is of thy listless dreaming born.
The plow, the loom, the workman's shop,
   Are well, for man is half of earth;
But music, song, the finer arts,
   Have yet a more exalted worth.

A poet roamed the clover fields,
   Where brawny workmen tossed the hay
And sang their mellow mowing-songs,
   From early dawn till evening gray ;
And, as he idly passed along,
   The harvesters began to shout
And taunt the dreamy looker-on,
   For he was deemed a worthless lout.

But ah! the poet gathered more
   Of good to mortals than they knew,
From scented fields and sunny slopes
   And over-reaching skies of blue;

The song he wrought that summer day
    Was so replete with highest thought
That none might read its glowing lines
    Unaided by the strength they brought.

'T were libel on the human race
    To say it needed nothing more
Than what might minister to sense—
    The food it ate, the clothes it wore.
Whoe'er refines the human heart,
    Whoe'er expands the human mind,
Must needs be reckoned by the wise
    A benefactor to his kind.

Had Terence always been a slave
    He might have reached a riper age,
But Rome had never felt his power
    To lash her vices through the stage.
Was he more useful when he ran
    In haste to bring Lucanus wine,
Than when he taught the Latin race
    To make existence more divine?

No doubt the men of Sirmio thought
    Catullus worthless to his race,

With only skill to frame an ode
    In praise of Lesbia's form and face.
But when the French sacked Italy,
    Then learned they to respect his name—
Their homes were spared, their lives were saved,
    By reason of their poet's fame.

Then, poet, when the grosser world
    Derides thy soft and subtle art,
Be not ashamed, but feel that thou
    To human progress giv'st thy part.
If on Aonia's flowery steeps
    Thy reverent feet have softly trod,
Returning, they have brought to man
    The brightest benisons of God.

FOREBODINGS.

I could not see a lovely flower
   Expand its blossoms to the air,
And know that some ungenial blast
   Would blight its blooms and leave it bare,
And never feel a pang of pain
For loveliness so brief and vain;

I could not see a shining star
   Go dancing on its path at night,
And know that, like the Pleiad lost,
   'T would fall and vanish from our sight,
And never feel a keen regret
For brightness doomed so soon to set.

O flower of youthful tenderness!
   O beaming star of boyish trust!
Supremely beautiful art thou,
   But well I know thou too art dust:
And deeply in my heart I rue
The wreck the years will make of you.

The hand that gives so gladly now,
   The tongue whose words are pure and high,

And oh! the kind and gentle glance
　　That trembles from your tender eye.—
'T were richly worth a mine of gold
If they could last till you were old!

But you will learn to grasp and hoard;
　　The world will teach your tongue to lie;
And cold and hard will be the look
　　That age will fasten in your eye:
No blighted flower or fallen star
Could leave its first estate so far.

Such tears as old Urania wept
　　For bright Hyperion's darkened fate,
Such tears as Dante shed to see
　　Francesca's changed and sad estate,
Such bitter and regretful tears
I weep, when looking down the years.

For then that beauty will be marred
　　Which in your youth so brightly shone;
Your love of truth and right be lost,
　　And all your winning graces flown;
In manhood's prime you may not claim
A maiden conscience, void of shame.

The faded flower, the fallen star,
　　The broken branch, the withered leaf,—
Whatever bright and lovely was,
　　But has decayed—is food for grief;
But sadder blight may yet be thine
When virtue fades at youth's decline.

THE ANCIENT STILE,

REMOVED FROM THE VILLAGE GRAVEYARD, IN DECAY, AND A
GATE PUT IN ITS PLACE.

The heart's affections often twine
  About the least of earthly things,
And o'er an uncouth object love
  A thousand fancied graces flings ;
And thus it was that I had grown
  To deem the old, decaying stile
A thing as grateful to the sight
  As though 't were some palatial pile.

In infancy my shoeless feet
  Had pressed around it in my play,
For all the world seemed brighter there,
  And there I loved the most to stay ;
And in and out among the tombs
  I ran and romped till out of breath ;
For I knew naught of sacrilege,
  And I was ignorant of death.

And when the days of boyhood came,
  And boyish ties and dreams arose,

I often sat with some dear friend
   Upon those steps at evening's close,
And while the summer sunset spread
   Its flaming banners in the west,
With hopes as bright my spirit glowed,
   And lofty longings filled my breast.

And in the graver, later years,
   When hope had given place to care,
And all the good that was to be
   Had vanished for the ills that were,
I still delighted most to seek
   That quiet spot for sober thought,—
For all the peace the tombs could give,
   For all the lessons that they taught.

O tombs! a potent charm is yours
   To calm the troubled breast of man,
You awe the bold and check the rash
   As neither priest nor censor can ;
No mortal mind on evil bent
   Durst venture in your threatening shade,
But you afford a sure retreat
   From all the errors sin has made.*

* This stanza was probably suggested by the sentiments in " The Invo-
cation " to Volney's Ruins, which the author read some years ago.

Ah, yes! about that ancient stile
    A host of varied memories clung
Of boyish loves and boyish faiths,—
    The bright delusions of the young;
And memories of still deeper dye,—
    Remembered hours of pain and gloom,
Of questions weighed and faults deplored
    In the dread presence of the tomb!

Improvement is the aim of man;
    The old must vanish for the new;
And what is fresh and strange to us
    A younger race with love will view:
But on my mind this truth has dawned,
    And changes sad have stamped it in,
The New can never be to us
    As precious as the Old has been.

MODESTY.

How hard the lot of woman is
  When she to love's assault is prey,
And sees the idol of her dreams
  Unheeding pass her day by day!
And feels that, if a sigh or word
To tell her love, by him were heard,
Responsive passion might be stirred.

How hard, when yet her maiden mind,
  As chaste as snowy lily leaves,
Disdains to spin the cunning web
  Which love about its captive weaves,
And she apart in modest wise.
Elects to stand, with dreamy eyes
In whose soft depths such sadness lies.

'T is sad that such should be her fate;
  And yet, for all love's wild delight,
Its warm caress, its close embrace,
  Its sated sense of touch and sight,
I would not give that modest thought—

That scorn of hearts by intrigue caught—
That woman's longing to be sought.

Oft have I seen neglected maids,
  Pale in the shadow of their grief,
Like some blanched vine that yearns to feel
  The sun's hot kisses on its leaf,
And I have loved their modest mien,
And I have marked them, all unseen,
With pride and admiration keen.

Of womanhood this is the charm
  That makes her more than earthly sweet;
For this some great Olympian god
  Might bow to earth and kiss her feet;
For she is more than human then;
Divinity surrounds her when
She so exceeds the strength of men.

THE FLOWERS.

O beautiful roses, so queenly and fragrant!
  O sweet little violets, purple and shy!
O wild trailing creepers, abandoned and vagrant!
  I love every blossom beneath the blue sky!

When ardently suing for earth's brightest treasure,
  Sweet, friendly assistants I found them to be;
Each petal that danced at the gay Zephyr's pleasure
  A tongue was to utter love's pleading for me.

The angel Sandalphon the Talmud discloses,
  Transforming the prayers which the devotees moan
Into beautiful garlands and bright colored posies
  To bear in this guise to the foot of the Throne.

Not so in my courtship. *There* love changed the flowers
  To seraphs, and sent them (an eloquent band)
To plead with the might of their angelic powers
  For favor to me from the Queen of the Land.

Yes, lilies and roses depicted love's phases,
  And blushing carnations discoursed of its pains;

I sent from the woodlands the blue-bells and daisies,
   And murmured of love with the grass of the plains.

Oh, then as I plucked them, bright hope whispered
      plainly,
"Some day you shall cull them to offer your bride;"
But pleadings were futile, and hope whispered vainly,
   Her lover I was, and am nothing beside.

And now as I wander, unloved and rejected,
   I gaze on the flowers with a tender regard;
They brighten a spirit forlorn and dejected,
   And soften a path which the fates have made hard.

ŒDIPI.

Thou grand magician of the Grecian stage,
 Thou who possessed the master's lofty art
To paint the passions on the glowing page
 And stir the deep emotions of the heart,
To thy impassioned *Œdipus* we owe
The darkest picture of a mortal's woe.
A man o'erwhelmed by dark, resistless fate,
Foredoomed the foulest deeds to perpetrate,
Albeit his heart was innocent of guile
And loved the good and hated all the vile.
A curse the Sybils uttered at his birth
Foretold that his career upon the earth
Should be to walk, as in distempered sleep,
Through lowering glooms and dire abysms deep,
Treading such depths of sorrow, shame and woe
As Hades hath not for the shades below!
And so it was.   Engaged in manly strife,
Unconsciously he took his father's life;
He saved his country from disaster dread,
And, for reward, did his own mother wed.
Beguiled to such dark acts by cruel fate,
The knowledge of them made him desolate;
O'erwhelmed, appalled, distracted with his grief,
Death only gave his troubled breast relief.

O Sphinx, revisit now the Phiceon hill !
  We mortals have a riddle to propound,
And if the Muses teach thee mysteries still,
  Mayhap to it an answer thou hast found :
How may the being without power of sight
Be conscious how to guide his steps aright?
And how the creature of enfeebled arm
Have strength to shield his puny frame from harm ?
We see, in all the ages of the world,
Men tost by fate, like dead leaves, lightly whirled
By eddying winds. Without an evil thought,
False steps they take, and are to ruin brought;
Or, seeing all the dangers hovering round,
They have not strength to reach the safer ground.
Hereditary passions sway the soul,
And o'er their victims heavy shadows roll;
And ties of kinship and of friendship throng
Life's path with woes wrought by another's wrong;
And beauty, grace and virtue are the mark
For envy's sting and hatred's intrigues dark.
Not theirs the fault, but theirs the bitter pain,
For on their brows Fate writes the curse of Cain—
Despised, abhorred, in abject misery
They dwell apart—earth's fated Œdipi !

Of one we read, in rank and beauty great,
  A child of golden hopes, whose dreams were all

Delusions painted by deceitful fate,
  Alluring her to most disastrous fall!
Of queenly presence, and a face divine,
A fancy brilliant as Golconda's mine,
Unconscious sorcery of voice and air,
Entrapping hearts as with a Circe's snare;
A nature happy as a rippling rill,
With French caprices, but an English will;
A heart whose fervid currents learned to flow
Where strong emotions in warm bosoms glow;
And that imperial boon, a double crown :
These fatal gifts hurled Marie Stuart down!
Ambitious courtiers, England's envious queen,
Her own rash favors, Darnley's jealous spleen,
And hateful calumny's envenomed tongue,
Around her path such dire misfortunes flung
That she, " the soft Medusa," at whose cry
A thousand swords once from their sheaths would fly,
And whose sweet nature was as Dian's pure,
Must insult, wrong and bondage all endure;
Dethroned, defamed—at last Fate kindly gave
A boon—if 't was a boon—an alien grave!

And he who towered his fellow men above,
  Burdened with gifts whose very splendor killed
Those cherished flowers, contentment, faith, and love,
  Wherewith the humbler mortal's path is filled;

By fate impelled, he, Phœnix-like, did start
The very fires which were to sear his heart!
He, like a base conscript iconoclast
In fate's employ, did his own fortunes blast!
His pride, his lust, his scorn of man and Heaven,
Were by transmission from his fathers given;
And that these poisonous seeds might thrive apace,
And bear rich fruit of sorrow and disgrace,
Fate fostered them with a malicious care.
Unhappy Byron! lord of earth and air,
Whose genius stooped to kiss the lowliest flowers,
Or soared aloft to bask in splendid showers
Of Eden's sunlight! Oh, had fate been kind,
And to thy brilliant faculties of mind
Had added pure and steady moral powers,
Thy life had been one chain of golden hours!
But thou wast doomed, who gave to England fame
And gave thy life in freedom's sacred name,
A mental Ajax in a moral night,
With inward faults and outward foes to fight.

But why should I attempt to single out
   The famed whose fate has been the most unkind?
'T is not the great alone; the obscure lout
   Must also tread life's devious journey blind.
How many souls have struggled to subdue
Some evil appetite, that ever drew

Them deeper down to infamy and shame!
How many breasts, all innocent of blame,
Have burst with grief for wicked actions done
By those whose fortunes and their own were one!
O Life! O Fate! I contemplate with pain
The flowers that languish for the summer rain;
The poor caged birds, that are too sad to sing,
Denied the power to soar upon the wing;
And the green trees, so grand, erect, and tall,
Which in the fury of the tempest fall—
But, saddest of all thoughts! that man should be
The toy, the puppet of fatality!
His mind, his strength, his joys, his golden dreams,
Like bubbles broken upon ruffled streams!
His hope expanding, like a lovely flower,
Only to fade in an unhappy hour!
His aims perverted and his labors marred
By the misfortunes of the evil-starred!

www.ingramcontent.com/pod-product-compliance
Lightning Source LLC
Chambersburg PA
CBHW020041030726
47499CB00007B/2535